READY ALL THESE

NATE THE GREAT

DETECTIVE STORIES
BY MARJORIE WEINMAN SHARMAT
WITH ILLUSTRATIONS BY MARC SIMONT:

Includes Detective Tips & Activities!

Nate The Great and me

The Case of the Fleeing Fang

by Marjorie Weinman Sharmat

illustrations by Marc Simont

Delacorte Press

Published by
Delacorte Press
Bantam Doubleday Dell Publishing Group, Inc.
1540 Broadway
New York, New York 10036

Visit us on the Web! www.bdd.com
**Educators and librarians, visit the BDD Teacher's Resource Center at
www.bdd.com/teachers**

Library of Congress Cataloging-in-Publication Data

ISBN 0-385-32601-7
Cataloging-in-publication data is available from the Library of Congress.

The text of this book is set in 18-point Goudy Old Style.
Book design by Trish Parcell Watts
Manufactured in the United States of America
October 1998
10 9 8 7 6 5 4 3 2 1

For my dog, Dudley, who _ _ _ _ _ _*
at the right time
and gave me the solution to this case.

—M.W.S.

*ATTENTION, DETECTIVES!
WHAT IS THE MISSING WORD
IN THIS DEDICATION?

(The answer is somewhere in this book.)

Chapter One

Happy Detective Day!

My name is Nate the Great.
I am a detective.
My dog, Sludge, is a detective too.
We have solved many cases.
Many, many, many cases.
Would *you* like to solve
a case with me?
Would *you* like to be
a detective too?
Good.

Because I have a case to solve.
Right now.
Before the ice cream in front of me
turns to mush.
Collapses.
Before I have to slurp
strawberry soup.
Are you ready?
Our case starts
when the ice cream
was young and healthy.
My doorbell rang.
I opened the door.
I saw a row of people and pets:
Rosamond and her four cats.
Oliver and his eels.
Finley and his rat.

Pip.
Esmeralda.
Claude.
Annie.
Annie's brother, Harry.
"Surprise!" they yelled.
"Happy Detective Day!"
Rosamond spoke up.
"We are having a
detective party just for you.
Because you have solved
so many cases for us."

A GOOD DETECTIVE HAS TO NOTICE THINGS.
THINGS THAT ARE THERE.
AND NOT THERE.
HAVE YOU NOTICED ANYTHING YET?

Rosamond was holding two big boxes.
"Look!" she said.
"A box of strawberry ice cream
and a box of tuna fish pancakes."
"Tuna fish pancakes?" I said.
"I, Nate the Great, love pancakes,
but . . ."
"My cats, Super Hex, Big Hex,
Little Hex, and Plain Hex,
love these pancakes," Rosamond said.
"And that is why
they should eat
all of them," I said.
Rosamond stepped inside.
"We surprised you," she said.

10

"You, the great detective,
didn't have a *clue*
that we were coming.
Ha ha ha."
Rosamond has a strange laugh.
That is no surprise.
Everyone was laughing.
Except Annie.

She looked sad.
"Fang wanted to come," she said.
Annie is always with Fang.

DID YOU NOTICE THAT FANG WASN'T THERE?

12

Chapter Two

Where Is Fang?

"**W**here *is* Fang?" I asked.

"He ran away," Annie said.

Rosamond nodded. "Now you have
a new case," she said.

"Nate the Great Finds Fang."

I, Nate the Great,

did not want to do that.

Fang's teeth get bigger every day.

Esmeralda spoke up.

Esmeralda is wise.

"Nate can't solve cases today.
This is his day off."
"No problem," I said.
"I will teach all of you
how to be a detective.
I will teach you how
to find Fang. Come in."

WHAT WOULD YOU DO FIRST TO FIND FANG?

I, Nate the Great, said to Annie,
"First you have to *remember*.
Remember if there was
anything different
about Fang today.
Any reason why he might run away.
Then remember where you last saw him.
Remember what he was doing.
Remember who was there."

Annie said, "I got Fang ready
for the party.
I didn't have time to give
him a bath.
So I feather-dusted him."
"You *feather-dusted* him?"
"Yes. It makes his fur
nice and clean."

WOULD YOU WANT TO BE A FEATHER-DUSTED DOG?
DO YOU THINK FANG RAN AWAY FROM ANNIE
BECAUSE SHE DUSTED HIM?
WHEN SOMEBODY IS MISSING,
THINK ABOUT <u>WHY</u>.
PUT YOURSELF IN A DOG'S SHOES. PAWS. WHATEVER.

"Very well," I said.

"Fang is clean. What else?"

"Fang was going to do
a trick for your party,"
Annie said. "I have been
teaching him commands."

"How?"

"I've got a rhyming book for dogs.
Each line is a new command.
The first is *Do a trick.*
The second line is
Lick, lick, lick.
Then there's a new rhyme.
Stop and wait.

16

Go to the gate.
Then there's another rhyme.
Go to the park
and—"
"Ho hum," Rosamond said.
"My cats can do all sorts of tricks."
"Well, Fang knows all the rhymes,"
Annie said. "But he mixes them up.
When I say the first line
he does the second.

Instead of tricks,
he licks, licks, licks."
Annie grinned.
"But I solved *that* problem.
I just say the *second* line.
Lick, lick, lick.
And then Fang does the trick!"
"Good thinking," I said.
"Yes," Annie said. "And it
works for all the rhymes.
Like *gate* and *wait* and—"
"Ho hum again," Finley said.

ARE DOG RHYMES AND FEATHER-DUSTING CLUES?
I DON'T KNOW YET.
IF YOU KNOW,
THEN PERHAPS YOU HAVE ALREADY
SOLVED THIS CASE.
AND I, NATE THE GREAT,
WILL NEED TO TAKE
DETECTIVE LESSONS FROM YOU.

I looked at Annie.
"Where is the last place
you saw Fang?"
"Well, Harry, Fang, and I
were on our way to your house.
We were at the corner of
Dartmouth Street and Oakdale Street.
All of a sudden two tiny poodles
came up to Fang.
They started to bark.

19

Fang looked surprised.
So I tried to shoo the poodles away.
I barked right back at them.
Bark! Bark! Bark!"
"Then what?" I asked.
"Then Fang ran off," Annie said.
"He ran down Dartmouth Street.
We went after him,
but he was too fast."
"Was he running after the poodles?"
I asked.
"No, they just stood there.
I think he was running away
from them."

"Let me get this straight,"
I said. "Fang is ten times bigger,
stronger, and toothier
than two tiny poodles.
And he was *afraid* of them?"
"Yes," Annie said.

YOU HAVE A JOB TO DO.
GET A PIECE OF PAPER
AND DRAW A PICTURE
OF A HUGE, FANGY DOG
RUNNING AWAY FROM
TWO TINY POODLES.
THEN PRINT BELOW IT:
"WHAT IS WRONG WITH THIS PICTURE?"

Chapter Three

Green Hair and Fluffy-Bunny Shoes

I, Nate the Great, raised my voice.
"Has anybody else seen Fang?" I asked.
Rosamond spoke up.
"I am in charge of this case.
I am the head detective.
Direct your answers to me."

Pip raised his hand.
Pip hardly ever says anything.
"I saw Fang," he said.
"On the way over here.
On Dartmouth Street.
He was following a lady
in a green hat."

"Following?" Oliver said.
"Good for him.
I believe in following.
I'll follow anybody."
I, Nate the Great,
already knew that.
Oliver is a pest.
But he learns things.
"Have you ever followed the lady
in the green hat?" I asked.
"Do you know where she lives?"
"I have followed her
from store to store,"
Oliver said. "But I don't know
where she lives."
"Has anybody else ever seen this
lady who wears a green hat?"
I asked.

"Yes," said Finley.

"She wears a rose in her ear."

"Her hair is green too," Claude said.

"And her shoes look like fluffy bunnies."

WHAT DO YOU THINK OF THIS ROSIE-POSIE,
GREEN AND FLUFFY INFORMATION?
SOMETIMES DETECTIVES GET MORE
INFORMATION THAN THEY WANT.
BUT A DETECTIVE CAN'T BE TOO PROUD.
I, NATE THE GREAT, LISTEN TO EVERYTHING.

I said, "A rose in her ear?
Green hair?
Fluffy-bunny shoes?
This sounds very strange."
Rosamond looked mad.
"It doesn't sound strange to me,"
she said. "And this is my case."
Oliver tapped me on the shoulder.
"I can help," he said.
He pulled something from his pocket.
"Sometimes I take pictures
of people I follow," he said.
"Here is the lady in the green hat."

WE MIGHT HAVE A CLUE IN THIS PICTURE!
HINT: WOULD FANG LIKE ANY OF THESE BAGS?

"I, Nate the Great, say that
this lady buys many things
and carries them around.
Like meat.
Maybe Fang smelled her meat.
Dogs can smell things at a distance.
Fang might be following
the smell of meat."
"So if we find the lady,
we find Fang," Annie said.
Rosamond clapped her hands.
"My case is almost solved.
We can start the party soon.
This ice cream
is beginning to melt."
"I will put it in the freezer," I said.

"No!" Rosamond said. "If you
keep it out of the freezer,
it means we *must* solve
this case soon."
"I, Nate the Great, say it means
we will eat pink goo."

SHOULD THE ICE CREAM
GO INTO THE FREEZER?
NEVER MIND, THE ANSWER WON'T HELP THIS CASE.

Chapter Four
A Red Herring

Rosamond went into the kitchen,
put the box of ice cream
on the table,
and came back with pink fingers.
I said, "The lady in the green hat
could be a red herring."
"A red herring?" Rosamond gasped.
"My cats *love* red herring."
"No, not the kind you eat,"
I said. "It's something that can
seem like a clue,
look like a clue,
feel like a clue,
smell like a clue,
but isn't a clue."
"So, what do we do?" Annie asked.

"I, Nate the Great, say
that we have talked enough.
Now it is time to go out
and look for Fang."

"Look for Fang by himself," I said.
"Look for Fang and
the green-hat lady.
Go to the corner of Dartmouth Street
and Oakdale Street.
Go down Dartmouth Street.
Walk the same streets
Annie, Harry, and Fang
walked before they reached
the corner of Dartmouth Street
and Oakdale Street.

Go to their house
and see if Fang went back home."
"This will take forever," Rosamond said.
"Split up," I said.
"Decide who goes where.
And go in pairs.
So that you each have a helper."
"A helper?" Pip asked.
This must have been
Pip's big day for talking.
"Yes, it helps to have a helper.
I have a great one. Sludge."
"Can we take him with us?" Annie asked.
"I, Nate the Great, need him here."
"We're off!" Rosamond said.

THEY LEFT IN A HURRY.
THERE WAS NO TIME
TO GIVE THEM
ANOTHER DETECTIVE TIP.
BUT HERE IT IS.
EAT PANCAKES.
PANCAKES HELP ME THINK.
BONES HELP SLUDGE THINK.
IF YOU WANT TO THINK AND EAT WITH US,
LOOK FOR MY FAVORITE PANCAKE RECIPE.
YOUR CLUE: THE NUMBER 61

Chapter Five

Pancakes and
Dripping Ice Cream

I made pancakes.
I gave Sludge a bone.
We ate and thought.
We knew that Fang was last seen
following the lady
in the green hat.
She could be carrying meat.
Fang could want that meat.

But what if she wasn't
carrying meat?
What if Fang *happened*
to be behind her?
What if he wasn't really
following her?
Maybe she was important to this case.
Maybe she wasn't.
I knew that Fang
had to have a reason
to leave Annie and Harry.
I looked at Sludge.
Would he ever run off?
Maybe if somebody scared him.
But nobody scares Fang.
Fang scares everybody.
I was stuck.
"We are getting nowhere,"
I said to Sludge.

SHOULD I, NATE THE GREAT,
GO OUT AND LOOK FOR FANG?
WHAT DO YOU THINK?

I wrote a note to my mother.

Dear Mother,
I might go out on a case. I might not. But just in case I go out on a case I will be back.
Love,
Nate the Great

Sludge and I finished eating.
But now Sludge was licking.
Ice cream. It was dripping on him
from the table.
"You are supposed to be
helping me with this case," I said.
Sludge always helps with my cases.

But now he was too busy licking.
Or maybe he was . . . helping!
Was Sludge trying to tell me something?
Yes!

Licking was a clue.
That was what Sludge thought.
And now, that was what *I* thought!

WHAT DO YOU THINK?
WHAT IS IMPORTANT IN THIS CASE?
WHAT IS A REAL CLUE
AND WHAT ISN'T?
DECIDE!

Chapter Six

The Real Clue

I wrote another note.

Dear Annie, Harry,
Rosamond, Oliver, Claude,
Pip, Esmeralda and Finley,
I, Nate The Great, say that
my day off is now on.
Sludge and I will go
find Fang.
We will be back,
Love,
Nate The Great

Sludge and I went out.

We knew where we were going.

We went there.

We found Fang.

He was asleep.

He woke up.

He was glad to see us.

We were glad to see him.

I, Nate the Great,
never thought
that I would ever say that.
Sludge, Fang, and I started
back to my house.

WHERE DID WE FIND FANG?
THAT IS THE BIG QUESTION.
I HOPE YOU HAVE THE BIG ANSWER.

Everyone was waiting
at my house.
Everyone looked sad.
Sludge and I walked in.
Then Fang walked in behind us.
Annie yelled, "Fang!"
Annie and Harry
rushed toward Fang
and hugged him.
"My cats and I
could have found him,"
Rosamond said.
"I was born to be a detective."
Annie looked at me.
"*You* were born to be
a detective," she said.
"Where did you find Fang?"
"Sludge knew the big clue," I said.
"The clue was the mixed-up rhymes."

Annie looked puzzled.
"I, Nate the Great, say
that Fang must leave the room
while I explain this.
Or he will go crazy
when he hears
all the rhymed commands."
"I will put him in the kitchen,"
Annie said.

Annie was back in a minute.
I went on.
"You said that when
you say one line,
Fang does the
other line instead.
When the rhymes were
trick and *lick*,
Fang licked first.
Then you said *wait* and *gate*.
So Fang went to the gate
before he waited.
Then you said *park*.
But Rosamond stopped you
before you told us
what rhymed with *park*."
I looked around the room.
"What doggie rhyme
goes with *park*?"

"I'm too smart to answer
such an easy question,"
Rosamond said.
"We all know it's *bark*," I said.
"Right," Annie said. "The rhyme
was *park* and *bark*. Go on."
"When the two tiny poodles
went up to Fang and barked,
you said, 'Bark! Bark! Bark!'
Fang thought it was a command.
The command that rhymed with
Go to the park.
And that's where he went.
And that's where I found him.
I, Nate the Great, knew
that Fang would never be
afraid of two tiny poodles.
So he had to have another
reason to run away."

"You solved a case
on your day off,"
Esmeralda said.
"There's another thing
about this case," I said.
"Fang wasn't really missing."
I turned to Annie and Harry.
"*You* were!

Fang went where he thought
you told him to go.
He thought you would show up.
If Fang could talk,
he would tell you
that this was the Case of
the Missing Annie and Harry."
Rosamond clapped her hands.
"Now we can start our party."
She went into the kitchen.
"Fang has the ice cream.
All over him!" she said.
"You did not solve
this case fast enough.
At least we have the
tuna fish pancakes."

"Never mind," I said.
"I will make all of you detectives
my special pancakes.
They even have a special name."

HERE IS WHAT I MADE FOR MY FRIENDS:
LATKES
YOUR CLUE: THE NUMBER 62

I made stacks and stacks.
"At last we eat!" Rosamond said.
Everyone sat down.
"Happy Detective Day,
Nate the Great,"
Annie said.
"We're all detectives today,"
Rosamond said.
"We all worked hard."
"You're right," I said.
"In fact, there are more
detectives than you
know about."

YOU WORKED HARD TOO.
SO PLEASE WRITE DOWN
ON YOUR PIECE OF PAPER:
I SOLVED A CASE TODAY WITH NATE THE GREAT.
WE DID IT! NATE THE GREAT AND ME.

NOW COME IN. JOIN THE PARTY.
HAVE A PANCAKE OR TWO.

DETECTIVE CERTIFICATE

I, NATE THE GREAT, AWARD YOU,

— — — — — — — — — — — — ,

this Detective Certificate for
being a great helper on this case.
We have been through a lot together.
Red herrings, green hat, licks
and tricks.
I, Nate the Great, say never give up.
I will be back.
I will always be back.

Nate the Great

TIPS ON HOW TO BE A GREAT DETECTIVE
by *Nate the Great*

- First, you have to *think*.
- Second, it helps to have a helper.
  I have a great one.
  Sludge. But it's all right if you don't.
- You have to *remember*.
- You have to *notice*
  people, places, and things.
- You have to *look*
  for facts and clues.
- You have to ask questions.
- You have to
  take ideas apart
  and put them together again.
- You have to figure out
  what is important.
  And what isn't.

Here are some fun things to do
that can help you be
a better detective.
I, Nate the Great, say
that you should
have a grown-up help you.
Believe me, grown-ups can
be great detectives too.

UNSCRAMBLING A SECRET CODE

Sometimes it is important for a detective to leave a coded message. And sometimes a detective must unscramble a coded message to solve a case.

Each symbol matches up with a letter of the alphabet. Match them up correctly and you'll be well on your way to being a great detective!

SPOTTING A DISGUISE

Sometimes a detective has to go undercover. This means changing the way you look so that no one recognizes you.

Do you recognize these disguised people?

Now get a photograph of your mom, dad, brother, or sister. Place tracing paper over the photo and trace the image. Next, think up a disguise that would make it hard to know who the person is. Show your masterful makeover to the person in question and see if they recognize themselves.

A.

B.

C.

D.

USING INVISIBLE INK

Take a second look next time you see a blank piece of paper. It may not be as blank as it seems.

You may want to leave someone you know an invisible message.

You will need:

1. Lemon juice in a bowl.
2. A thin paintbrush.
3. White or pink paper.

Dip the paintbrush in the lemon juice and write something you don't want others to read. Wait for the paper to dry. *Poof!* What you wrote cannot be seen. Or can it? Hold the paper up to a bright light. What you wrote is now visible again!

GOOD NEWS! If you put lemon juice on pancakes, they won't disappear!

NATE'S PANCAKE RECIPE

Nate the Great loves to eat pancakes every time he works on a case.

Main Ingredient
One grown-up to help you

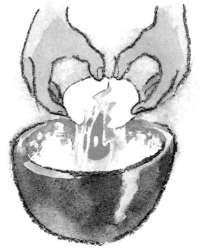

Ingredients
1-2/3 cups of milk
1 egg
2-1/2 tablespoons vegetable oil
1-1/2 cups flour
1-1/2 tablespoons sugar
1-1/2 teaspoons baking powder
1/2 teaspoon baking soda
1/2 teaspoon salt

1. Mix the milk, egg, and oil in a bowl.
2. In another bowl, combine the flour, sugar, baking powder, baking soda, and salt.
3. Pour the liquid ingredients into the dry ones.
4. Beat with a whisk until the mixture is smooth.
5. Lightly oil a pan and heat it.
6. Pour a small ladleful of batter into the hot pan. Spread into a circle.
7. Cook about 3 minutes on each side.
8. Repeat until you have a nice stack of pancakes.

Makes about 12 pancakes.

POTATO PANCAKES

Latkes—also called potato pancakes—are Nate the Great's special pancakes for special occasions.

Main Ingredient
One grown-up to help you

Ingredients
2 eggs
1/3 cup flour
1/4 cup grated onion
1/4 teaspoon ground black pepper
4 large potatoes, peeled and shredded
3 tablespoons butter

1. Combine the eggs, flour, onion, and pepper in a bowl.
2. Rinse the shredded potatoes and blot dry with a paper towel. Stir into the egg mixture.
3. Melt 1-1/2 tablespoons of the butter in a pan. Use medium heat.
4. Spoon 1/3 cup of the mixture into the pan. Spread into a circle.
5. Cook 3 minutes on each side, or until golden brown.

Makes 12 pancakes.
Serve with applesauce or sour cream.

Do you remember the missing word on page five?
Have you found the answer yet? It's . . .

BARKED

That's the missing word!
And because you worked hard to find the answer,
here's a treat just for you.

STRAWBERRY MILK SHAKE SURPRISE

Main Ingredient
One grown-up to help you

Ingredients
2 pints strawberry ice cream
4 cups milk
Ginger ale
Strawberries (optional)

1. Place ice cream in a large mixing bowl. Let it soften.
2. Add the milk and beat with an eggbeater until smooth.
3. Pour into tall glasses until halfway full.
4. Add ginger ale and stir.
5. Decorate with a strawberry.
6. Drink through a straw.

Makes 6–9 Milk Shake Surprises

Enjoy!

Marjorie Weinman Sharmat has written 130 books for children and young adults, which have been translated into seventeen languages. She lives with her husband, author Mitchell Sharmat, in Tucson, Arizona. They have two sons, Craig and Andrew.

Marc Simont won the Caldecott Medal for his artwork in *A Tree Is Nice* by Janice May Udry. He has illustrated all the Nate the Great books. He lives in West Cornwall, Connecticut.

249